I hope you always
have great friends!
Pat Canuteson

Herbie the Hamster Searches for Friends

Written by Pat Canuteson

© 1994 All Rights Reserved

Herbie the Hamster lived with two little girls.

Their names were Leah and Sarah.

Other pets in the house were a dog named Reebok,

Three fish, and a cat named Shasta.

Herbie's house was a large hamster cage.

He had plenty of room to play.

But, Herbie was lonely. He had no friends,

So, he wanted to run away.

One night, when the girls were sleeping,

Herbie opened his cage door.

"Finally, my chance to escape," Herbie said,

"There's a big world to explore."

Herbie climbed out of his cage and ran away

As fast as his legs could run.

"Who are you, and where are you going?"

Asked the fish in the aquarium.

"My name is Herbie, and I'm exploring the world.

I'm unhappy, and I'm looking for friends."

"You can find friends the world over," the fish said to Herbie,

"But true happiness comes from within."

"Come in and join us. We'll be your friends,"

The three fish said to him.

But, Herbie stood outside looking in at the fish.

"I'm sorry, but I can't swim."

15

Herbie was sad. He wanted friends just like him

To run, and laugh, and play.

He said, "Perhaps I'll come back and join you later."

Then, Herbie turned and walked away.

"Hello," a voice called out, "And whom might you be?"

Herbie looked, and there she sat.

"My name is Herbie the Hamster," he said.

She answered, "I'm Shasta the Cat."

"I'm exploring the world and looking for friends,"
Herbie said to Shasta the Cat.

"A hamster, you say?" was Shasta's reply,
"My, you're nice and fat!"

"What do you mean by that?" Herbie asked,

As he looked into Shasta's eyes.

"Oh, nothing," Shasta said as she licked her lips,

And, then, Herbie realized.

"It's alright to be different," Herbie tried to explain.

"There's no reason we can't be friends.

You can find friends the world over," Herbie said to Shasta.

"But, happiness comes from within."

"Yes, I know," said Shasta. "Would you like to be mine? I'm sure we could have lots of fun."

"I don't think I can trust you," Herbie said to Shasta.

Then, Herbie started to run.

Shasta jumped to her feet and ran after Herbie.

For her, it was only a jog.

They rounded a corner, and whom should they meet?

There stood Reebok the Dog.

Then, Shasta the Cat saw Reebok the Dog.

And quickly ran away.

"Why was she chasing you, friend?" Reebok asked.

Herbie looked up. "Friend, did you say?"

From that day on, Herbie the Hamster and Reebok the Dog

Became the best of friends.

And, Herbie learned as he grew older and wiser

That true happiness comes from within.

Herbie the Hamster learned another lesson that day.

That no matter how many friends you gain or lose,

It's alright to have friends that are different than you,

Just be careful of the friends you choose.

Edwards Brothers Malloy
Thorofare, NJ USA
April 3, 2013